POSSUM
and the PEEPER

Words and pictures by Anne Hunter

Houghton Mifflin Company
Boston 1998

The text of this book is set in 15 point Cochin.
The illustrations are watercolor, colored pencil, and ink, reproduced in full color.

Library of Congress Cataloging-in-Publication Data
Hunter, Anne.
Possum and the peeper / written and illustrated by Anne Hunter.
p. cm.
Summary: When Possum is awakened on the first day of spring
by a loud noise that won't stop, he and all the other animals,
who have also had their winter's sleep disturbed,
set out to discover who is making all the racket.
ISBN 0-395-84631-5
[1. Opossums—Fiction. 2. Frogs—Fiction. 3. Animals—Fiction.
4. Spring—Fiction.] I. Title.
PZ7.H916555Ph 1998
[E]—DC21 97-9470 CIP AC

Manufactured in the United States of America
HOR 10 9 8 7 6 5 4 3 2 1

To Forrest

Peep! Peep! Peep!

Possum opened one small eye. What was that noise?

He buried his head deeper in his warm winter nest.

Peep! Peep! Peep!

"I'll never get back to sleep with all that racket," he said. "I'm going to go find out who's being so inconsiderate so early in the spring."

Possum stepped out into the cool, green morning.

Peep! Peep! Peep!

Possum looked up.

A pair of catbirds were building their nest high in a tree among the new leaves.

"Is that you peeping up there?" demanded Possum.

"Not us," said the catbirds. "We can scarcely hear ourselves sing with all that clamor."

"Well, I'm going to go see for myself who's making such an awful din."

"We'll come, too," said the catbirds. "We can search high in the trees while you look low on the ground." They set off through the woods.

Possum stopped to sniff the
trout lilies blooming along the path.
Peep! Peep! Peep!
They followed the noise up a hill.

At the crest of the hill stood a
bear blinking blearily outside his cave.

"Who woke me from my warm winter
sleep?" he snarled, showing his long
white teeth.

"Was it YOU?" he said, spying Possum.

"No," said Possum, "but we are on our
way to find out who it was."

"I had better come along then," growled
the bear. "You may need someone of my
size when you find this fellow."

They continued over the hill, the catbirds flying overhead, the bear grumbling along behind.

The spring sun shone down warm on their feathers and fur.
Peep! Peep! Peep! The sound was getting louder and louder.

They came down to a marsh where they saw a muskrat spring-cleaning his house.

"Excuse us!" shouted Possum. "Have you been peeping?"

"**What?**" yelled the muskrat. "I can't hear you over all that noise!"

"Well, we're on our way to put a stop to it once and for all," said the bear, "if you could show us the way through this swamp."

They pressed on, following the muskrat, peering between new green

shoots and into dark pools. Closer and closer. Louder and louder.

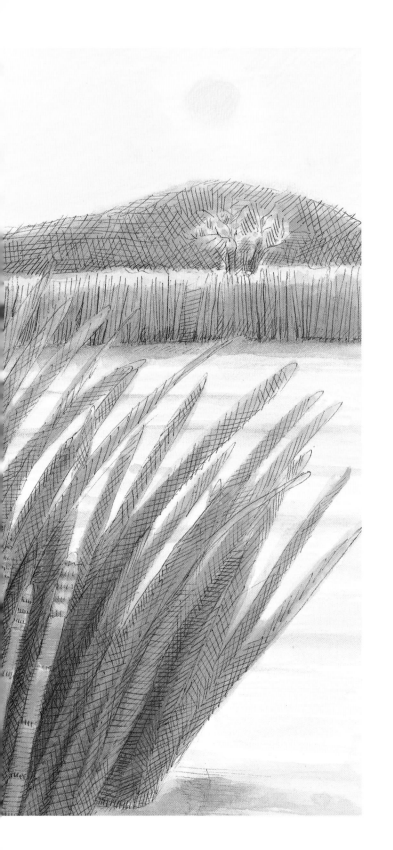

Possum pushed aside some reeds.

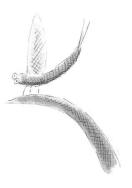

"**AH HA!**" they cried, squinting at a small spot on the bank.

"How could such a speck of a thing make such a huge racket?" asked the bear.

"You have woken up the entire forest, little frog," said Possum.

The little peeper looked up, from the possum to the muskrat to the catbirds and finally to the bear. Then he puffed out his tiny throat.

"**Rise and shine!**" he shouted. "**Shake a leg! Build your nests and clean your burrows! It's spring! It's spring! It's spring!**"

The bear stepped closer to the little frog. "I," he growled, "don't like to be awakened so early in the year, especially," he added, "by a frog."

"Oh, but look at the beautiful spring flowers," cried the peeper,
"and sniff the good spring smells. How could you want to sleep through
such a glorious spring day?"

The animals looked around at the budding trees. They smelled the

blooming flowers and felt the warm sun shining. They listened to the
buzzing bees and warbling birds. Legs stretched and bellies rumbled.
It was true, quite true. No one could deny that it was a fine thing
indeed to be out and about on the first warm day of spring.

"There's nothing quite like a good walk on a spring morning," proclaimed Possum. "Won't you join us for breakfast, little peeper?"

But the spring peeper was already peeping again at the top of his lungs. **"Time for breakfast! Toast and tea! The early bird gets the worm!"** **Peep! Peep! Peep!**

Peep! Peep! Peep!